SYLVANDER
Finds a Gift of True Happiness

Written by
Rispba McCray-Garrison

Illustrated by
Marvin Alonso

Sylvander Finds a Gift of True Happiness
Copyright © 2018 by Rispba McCray-Garrison

Dedication:

This is for **my beautiful children** who always inspire me, and constantly fill my life with joy and laughter. Always be the best that you can be and continue to grow in the Wisdom of God. I love you with all my heart

To my husband **David**, whose love, help and support encouraged me to complete and publish this children's book. You have constantly been a blessing to me.

To **my parents** and **my siblings**. Thank you so much for your encouraging words, your unconditional love and your support. You always made me believe that all things are possible with God.

Once upon a time, I think it was spring, there lived a strong and handsome fox named Sylvander. Sylvander lived in a city called Foxville that was located in the beautiful Northern Forest of Sharewood. Sylvander was regarded as one of the most important and wealthy foxes of Foxville.

Many of the foxes of the village looked up to Sylvander and considered him to be the most powerful and influential fox that ever lived.

With all of his power and greatness, Sylvander was not a happy fox. He was very lonely. Every day he would get out of bed and look at himself in the mirror for at least an hour. Now, Sylvander was not admiring or praising himself as he looked in the mirror, but he was trying to find a reason why he should get up and live his routine, boring life. Sylvander felt empty deep inside. He didn't feel the joy and happiness that was expressed among other foxes. Sylvander did not see himself as being important or loved.

After looking in the mirror, Sylvander gave a big sigh and began to prepare himself for the day. After he was dressed he sat down at the breakfast table, and gazed at his distorted reflection in the bowl that held his rabbit cereal. "Why do I feel so sad inside?" he said. "I'm not a bad looking fox, I have a great home, Foxes of the village respect me, and I have just about everything that any fox would want. Yet I feel like I'm a nobody......an outcast." Sadly, Sylvander ate his breakfast and left for work.

As Sylvander slowly walked to his company building, he practiced his every day "Hello", and his smile. As he passed by the foxes in the street, they would greet him with a wave or a "Hello sir", or "Good morning Sylvander". Sylvander responded to them with a friendly wave and "Hello".

While he was walking down Main Street, Sylvander passed by Roxie's Cafe. Now, Roxie's Cafe, for many years, had a reputation of being one of the dirtiest and disorderly Cafe's of Foxville. As he was passing the front door of the cafe, he accidentally bumped into a filthy and homeless fox that was standing in front of Roxie's Cafe. The homeless fox was so startled that he dropped the bottle that he was carrying in his hand. The bottle crashed to the ground. The glass, with a smelly pink liquid, flew everywhere.

"Now look what you did! That bottle cost me a buck fifty...I...I think." the homeless fox said to Sylvander.

"What I did?!!" screamed Sylvander "You're the one who wasn't watching where you were going, and look at this, you ruined a good suit!"

"Well excuse me Mr..... Mr..... Mr. whoever you are. I didn't mean to ruin your suit, in fact, I'll ... I'll give you seven dollars to have it cleaned!"

"I don't want your filthy money!" Sylvander yelled back.

"Besides, I'm late for work, and I do not have any time to deal with foxes like you! Get out of my way and go take a bath!"

As Sylvander rushed down Main Street towards his company building he heard the homeless fox scream out to him, "Why you rude fox you! You think that you are better than me by showing me no respect?! I bet you don't have any respect for ...for ... for yourself! Who do you think you are treat ... treating me like that?!!"

Those words rang in Sylvander's head as he opened the front doors to his company building. He reached the elevators and realized that he was shaking. When the elevator door opened on the ground floor, Sylvander stood still and did not enter the elevator; instead, he watched the doors of the elevator close. Slowly, he turned around and started to cry. He couldn't believe that the words of the homeless fox had affected him.

Suddenly, Sylvander threw down his briefcase and ran out of the building. He ran as fast as he could through the city. He passed office buildings, he passed restaurants, he passed schools, he passed neighborhoods, and he passed everything that was in Foxville. Sylvander kept running until he was too tired to run anymore. Not being bothered about where he was, he fell to the ground and cried himself to sleep.

Suddenly, Sylvander was awakened by the sound of distant barking. He looked around and realized that he was in the deep green forest that surrounded Foxville. Sylvander wanted to go home. He was very hungry and very scared, but he could not remember which direction he needed to go in order to return to Foxville. The barking that had awakened him was getting closer. Sylvander was so confused and scared that he did not know what to do. Then, to his surprise, a deer ran past him and some birds flew by.

All of a sudden, a whole lot of animals of the forest ran, hopped, leaped, and flew right past Sylvander. The barking noise was coming closer and closer and closer. Sylvander became so scared that he started running also. He didn't know where he was going, but he just kept running and running. He finally stopped at a small flowing brook and looked around. "Oh, I'm never going to find my way home now. I just wish someone could help me and give me some food," he said to himself.

Then suddenly, a fat, brown, and delicious looking rabbit came hopping out of the forest. It hopped over to the flowing brook and started to drink the water. Sylvander looked at the rabbit and licked his lips. "Oh boy! Oh boy! I am in luck!" he softly said. He slowly crouched down and started creeping, ever so quietly across the brook towards the rabbit. The barking behind Sylvander was getting closer, but he paid no attention. He was determined to catch this beautiful and fat rabbit. When he was close enough to pounce on his prey, the rabbit suddenly looked up and noticed Sylvander.

Before Sylvander could pounce on the rabbit, the rabbit turned around and started running for his life. Now, Sylvander wasn't too pleased about this. So, he started running after the rabbit through the forest. Sylvander used every ounce of his strength to catch up with the rabbit, and finally, with one single leap he pounced right on top of him. He pinned the rabbit down and was getting ready to take his first bite when all of a sudden the rabbit screamed out and said, "OH, PLEASE DON'T EAT ME KIND SIR! I'M TOO SMALL FOR YOU, PLUS, I HAVE A FAMILY THAT LOVES ME! OH, OH PLEEEEEEASE HAVE MERCY!".

"Have mercy on you?! Give me one reason why I shouldn't eat you!" said Sylvander.

"Well...Well I.... Well, you see I can save your life."
"Save my life? YOU a RABBIT save my LIFE! I don't think so."
"Oh, but I can, sir. I can! You see, right now your life is in great danger, because you are being hunted by huge men on horses and their fierce dogs. Now, when they catch you, you are dead meat, I say DEAD MEAT. Therefore, by eating me you are risking your life, because I am the only one who can save you."

"Men on horses! Dogs! I think you're trying to trick me, and I don't believe any of this nonsense." "Oh sir, you need to believe me, because those barking noises behind us ARE the dogs. Now, if you follow me, I will save you. So pleeeeeeese let me go. We are running out of time!"

Sylvander released the rabbit, and the rabbit darted out into the forest. Sylvander followed the rabbit. The rabbit led him across logs, through grassy fields, under bushes, through hollow trees, across flowing brooks, through a swamp, and into a grassy hole. The hole was a tunnel that led way under ground. When they reached the end of the tunnel, there was a little burrow that was nicely furnished and decorated. A delicious scent coming from the kitchen reached Sylvander's nose. He was tired and out of breath. He felt like he was going to faint.

The rabbit offered him a chair and told him to sit down. Once Sylvander was seated, the rabbit said, "I have to go back out again. You make yourself comfortable, and I'll be back in a few minutes."

"But, where are you going? Those dogs might catch you and kill you." Sylvander said.

"Well, I have to direct the dogs away from my home because they are following our scent. Don't worry, I've been doing this for years." And after saying that, the rabbit dashed into the tunnel, which lead to the outside.

Sylvander could not believe what was happening to him. He had never witnessed this odd yet kind behavior. He leaned back in his chair and gave a big sigh. Suddenly, he heard barking coming from afar. He leaped out of his chair and hit his head on the ceiling. When he fell to the ground, he stayed there and listened. As he listened, he realized that the barking wasn't getting louder; instead, it got softer and softer and softer until there was silence in the air.

"He did it!" Sylvander said, "He really did it." Sylvander picked himself off the floor and sat back into the chair. He closed his eyes and smiled. Suddenly the rabbit dashed through the door and slammed it behind him. He was breathing hard. He leaned against the door and looked at Sylvander.

"Wow, that was rough. I think I'm getting too old for this. Anyway, we are safe now. Would you like anything to eat or drink?"

"Sure, thank you very much." said Sylvander," I'm very happy that you made it back safely. I thought maybe they had caught you."

"No, they will never catch me because I'm too fast and too smart. Please, sit down and have some tea and carrot cookies. I'm sorry that I don't have any meat. I'm a vegetarian."

"Thanks, but you've done more than enough. I'll eat something when I get home...that's if I can find my way back to Foxville."

"Don't worry, I'll show you the way back to Foxville. I know these forests inside and out. When the sun begins to set, I will take you to the path that will lead you safely to your village. But, for now let's just relax."

Sylvander and the rabbit talked and laughed for hours. When it was time to leave, the rabbit took Sylvander to a big hill that overlooked the forest. From a distance the sun was setting behind the trees. As the sky began to change colors, Sylvander could see Foxville sitting peacefully in the valley of the forest.

"Well, I guess this is it, my friend," said the rabbit. "All you have to do is follow that dirt path which will take you safely to your village".

"Thank you for everything. I don't know what I would have done without you. By the way, didn't you say that you have a family?"asked Sylvander.

"Yes, I do have a family. Well... I did have a family. They were all eaten by foxes a few years ago. I'm the only survivor. But, that is history and it is in the past. I know that my family is still with me, because their memories live within my heart. Now that, my friend, always keeps me looking towards the future. Here...I want you to have something. It has always brought me good luck and happiness," said the rabbit.

The rabbit pulled out a golden carrot and handed it to Sylvander. As Sylvander took the carrot, he looked the rabbit in his eyes and said, "You are the best friend that I've ever had. Thank you. I will never forget you."

"Well, you better get going because it's getting dark. Take care of yourself Sylvander. Maybe we will meet again someday".

"Maybe, my friend", replied Sylvander with a smile.

As Sylvander began running down the path, he suddenly stopped. He turned around and yelled, "I don't even know your name!"

"Lucky!" yelled the rabbit as he hopped away. "Thanks Lucky!" yelled Sylvander.

Sylvander started running towards Foxville when he suddenly tripped over a rock and was knocked unconscious. When he woke up he looked around and realized that he might have been dreaming. He picked himself up from the ground and brushed off his suit. When he turned around to head back towards Foxville, he saw a rabbit sitting by some bushes. "He looks like Lucky," he said to himself. Sylvander slowly approached the rabbit. Before he could say anything the rabbit, in fear, darted into the forest. A little surprised, Sylvander turned towards Foxville and started walking. For some reason he felt so happy that he started whistling a tune.

When Sylvander reached his company building, he went inside and yelled at the top of his lungs with a smile on his face. "Daddy's Home*!!!*" He got into the elevator, pushed the button for the twentieth floor and danced a jig as the elevator doors closed. When he reached the floor of his office, and after the elevator doors opened, he happily yelled out "Everyone stop what you are doing. Take two days off if you want, and ..everyone is getting a double raise on their salary."

Sylvander's employees turned around and looked at him in amazement. Confused they started whispering amongst themselves. As Sylvander headed towards his office his secretary approached him.

"Excuse me sir, but are you feeling ... Oh, I'm sorry. What I mean is did ... did you just say that everyone here is getting a double ... double raise?"

"That's exactly what I said. I also said that everyone may go home if they want to and take two days off! Now, if anyone has a problem with that, they can come see me in my office and we'll talk. Oh, hold all of my calls until tomorrow."

Sylvander smiled as he opened the doors of his executive office. After he had closed the doors behind him, he deeply inhaled and slowly exhaled.

"Yippee!!" He shouted with joy as he leaped up in the air. "This is a great day and a new beginning of my life!" As he danced over to his desk he noticed that the sun was still setting, and that he had missed most of the day. With a smile he jumped into his large chair, and swung himself around to watch the sun hide behind the hills of the forest. As Sylvander watched the sunset, he felt an object in his front pocket. He reached in and pulled out a golden carrot. In amazement he noticed an engraving on each side of the carrot that read:

Love, Trust, Loyalty. Forever

With a tear in his eye, Sylvander gazed out the window of his office while the sun hid behind the hills of the Sharewood Forest. As the sky slowly turned color from gold to magenta, he thought of Lucky and how he saved Sylvander's life.

"Thank you my dear friend," he whispered with a sigh "...thank you."

The End